MOUNTAIN MAN'S MUSE

MEN OF MAPLE MOUNTAIN BOOK FOUR

SADIE KING

LET'S BE BESTIES!

A few times a month I send out an email with new releases, special deals and sneak peeks of what I'm working on. If you want to get on the list I'd love to meet you!

You'll even get a free short and steamy romance when you join.

Sign up here:
www.authorsadieking.com/free

MOUNTAIN MAN'S MUSE

MEN OF MAPLE MOUNTAIN BOOK FOUR

He watches her through his lens, his craving for her growing, until he must act...

The moment I saw Heather down the lens of my camera, I knew she was mine.

With my camera, I follow her, my obsession growing.

Her curves, her lips, her smile—they all speak to me down the lens, as I build a private portfolio. An entire room in the basement devoted to her image.

When I finally get her in my studio, she ignites a passion that we both crave, giving me everything I ever wanted and making my life full.

She'll never know about the basement, about what's behind the locked door.

Will she?

Mountain Man's Muse is a soft stalker, mountain man romance featuring an OTT hero and the curvy girl who becomes the object of his obsession.

PROLOGUE

KANE

A cold ache spreads through my legs as I crouch in the scrub with my camera poised. There's a scratching noise in the bushes in front of me, and I carefully adjust my lens, getting ready to snap the animal that comes out of it.

Three nights I've camped on the edge of Maple Mountain tracking a male bobcat. Three days I've spent hidden in the brush with my camera ready.

I've photographed the local foxes and squirrels, but the bobcat remains elusive.

The bush moves, and a field mouse scurries out. It pauses, a berry in its paws, and I snap a few pictures. It's not the bobcat I've been tracking, but it'll earn me a few dollars from the right photography sites.

The mouse's ears twitch, and it scampers away in a hurry as if something has startled it. A moment later, I hear human footsteps.

From my position on the ridge, I swivel my camera downwards to the walking path below.

A blue cap comes into my field of vision, dark hair streaming out from underneath it. It's a woman—two women—but I keep my lens trained only on one.

She stops and turns to her friend, showing off the plumpest lips I've ever seen and deep green eyes sparkling with laughter at some joke I can't hear.

My breath hitches in my throat. She's beautiful.

Click

My finger hits the button before I know what I'm doing. I've got the long zoom lens on, and I'm far enough away that they don't hear the picture being taken.

Below the stunning face is a long neck. A droplet of sweat trickles down her throat, and I follow it with my lens down to the soft skin of her cleavage.

Heat rushes through my body like an electric shock. My blood heats as I watch the rise and fall of her breasts. She's panting hard from her climb up the path, her chest heaving up and down to a rhythm that matches the drum of my heart.

Adjusting my zoom, I pull out so I can see more of this beauty.

She's taller than average with wide hips and ass, thick thighs, and luscious curves. But it's her face I bring my lens back to. Those stunning lips. The innocent laughter.

I take another photo. And another. I've never done

this before, photographed people without their consent.

But she's not just anybody. I know that already with every fiber in my body. I know immediately that this woman is mine.

Mine.

Leaning against the rocks, she pulls a sandwich out of her backpack. This must be the end of their hike, and I watch as they eat and take pictures of the scenery.

I'm as hard as the rock around me, but I must wait. I'm used to waiting.

Silently, I photograph her. Getting to know her. Every angle, every look. I can't explain this need to capture her image.

Eventually, they pack up their food and head back down the trail. I wait until they're gone before I pack up my things and follow.

Already I know I'm not going back to my life before. As I follow her down the path, I'm already making plans. I'll sell my apartment; I'll find a place here, open a studio, and find a way to be with her.

My life is here now, on the mountain—with this woman.

HEATHER

Three weeks later…

The model stares out at me from the pages of the magazine with a nonchalant expression. I tilt my head and pout, wondering if I look as much like I don't give a shit about the world as she does. Although if I had skinny thighs like hers, I reckon I could get away with not giving a shit about anything.

I pinch my too big thighs.

Nope. These chunky flanks aren't going to let me get away with anything.

The bell above the coffee shop door tinkles, and I quickly shove the magazine under the counter.

"Good morning…" My voice falters when I see it's Kane, the wildlife photographer, and my chest flutters like there's a caged bird inside trying to get out.

Kane turned up in town a few weeks ago, and every

time he comes in the cafe, my tummy does little flips and my knees go like jelly.

Not to mention what happens to my lady bits. There's a tug, down there, that makes me squeeze my thick thighs together with longing.

Fumbling to put the magazine away, I meet his penetrating gaze.

"The usual?" I ask, trying to keep my voice calm so he doesn't know what effect he has on me. I mean, the guy is gorgeous—six foot something with shaggy dark hair and a wild beard.

Ursula, my bestie, says I should just ask him out, but what would a guy like that want with a chubby girl who works in a cafe?

He's a photographer, which sounds exotic and awesome, and I make coffee all day, which is dull and boring. Besides, if he was interested, he would have asked me out by now.

He fixes me with a smile that makes my insides melt.

"Sure."

I make his coffee slowly, taking my time grinding new beans and frothing the milk.

"How's the studio coming along?"

He's already told me about the cabin he bought on the edge of town and the studio he's building on-site. Why anyone would want to relocate to Maple Falls is beyond me. I've been stuck here my whole life, and I can confirm it's the most boring place on Earth.

Sure, I love the mountain, but even hiking gets boring after a while. I yearn for some excitement, something interesting to happen to take me away from my humdrum existence.

"It's almost finished."

His look is always intense, especially when he's talking about his work.

"So, what are you going to photograph up here?"

"You."

I cock my head; I must not have heard him right. Or he's making a joke. I decide it's a joke and laugh. "Because I'm such model material."

My eyes flutter, and I do a silly pose, like one of the models from the magazine. But he looks dead serious.

"Beauty comes in all forms." His blue eyes bore into mine, and the way he says it sets off tiny prickles of heat over my body.

Is he really suggesting I'm beautiful? This guy's delusional, or he's messing with me.

"Not according to fashion magazines."

"I wish you wouldn't read those." He sounds irritable, and I wonder how the hell he knows what magazines I read. Maybe he saw me stash *Cosmopolitan* under the counter.

I hand him his coffee, and he perches on one of the stools near the counter. He comes in here every day for a coffee and a chat. It's the highlight of my day, but I could never tell him that.

The bell above the door chimes, and a guy in hiking

gear comes in with a backpack slung over his shoulder. He must be a tourist visiting town. It's where half of our business comes from.

As he saunters up to the counter, his eyes run over my chest. My body tenses, but I try not to show it. I hate men staring at my boobs, but it comes with the territory of being a big girl. Big girl equals big boobs—which equals lots of unwanted staring.

"Can I help you?" I keep my voice light. It doesn't pay to get annoyed with customers; it's not good for business.

But Kane doesn't seem to have gotten the memo. He's staring at the man with a face like thunder. His fists are clenched, and there's a vein about to pop in his neck.

I'm not sure what's got him so rattled.

"I'm after something sweet."

The man leans on the counter and stares blatantly at my breasts as he says it.

"Eyes up, fuck head."

Kane's voice comes out gravelly and cold. The man turns toward him, and he must see that Kane means business because he holds his hands up in the air.

"Whoa, sorry man. Didn't know she was your woman."

"I'm not…" I start to speak, but Kane cuts me off.

"Get your coffee and get the fuck out."

The guy turns back to me, this time looking me in the eye. "Black coffee. To go."

My fingers fumble with the takeout coffee cup. I've never had a guy stand up for me like that before.

The birds in my chest beat their wings furiously. Not only is Kane hot, but he's also got the coolest job, and he just defended my honor. I think I'm in love.

You could cut the tension with a knife as I make the coffee. Kane keeps his eyes fixed on the man, who drums his fingers awkwardly on the counter. When I hand him his cup, he walks quickly out of the shop, Kane's narrow-eyed gaze following him.

"Um, thanks for that." I say.

Kane's gaze snaps back to me, and it's hard, intense, catching me off guard and making the tug in my core deepen.

"I hate to see assholes disrespecting women."

The flutter in my chest calms. I guess he would have done the same for anyone, not just for me.

Another customer comes in, and by the time I've finished serving them, Kane is gone.

Disappointment rolls over me. I must wait another whole day to see him again.

2

KANE

My fingers tap the mouse, clicking through the shots from today. There's Heather leaving her house, hair pulled high in a messy bun, her work uniform hugging her curvy figure.

The next shot is a close-up of Heather bending down to pat the neighbor's cat. Her full lips are slightly parted and pulled into a pouty smile.

There's a stirring in my pants as I look at her lips, her chest, her big round eyes. I can imagine those eyes looking up at me, those lips calling out my name as I sink into her.

The pressure in my pants is too much, and I unzip my fly. I give myself a hard stroke as I look at her face, imagining her lips wrapped around me.

One hand flicks through the photos: her skirt riding up her thighs as she walks to work; there's one where she's leaning on the counter, blurred through the glass, but I can make out the line of her cleavage. My other hand grips my shaft, sliding up and down, fantasizing about her legs wrapped around me.

I click back to the close-up, imagining those parted lips screaming my name.

My cock jerks out my release, spraying sticky cum into my palm. Squeezing my eyes shut to keep the image of Heather in my mind, I can almost feel her here with me.

I can feel her breath on my neck, her soft kisses on my mouth.

"I love you, baby girl."

Slowly, I open my eyes.

It's just me. Me in a cold, damp basement, sitting at a computer desk with my dick in my hand.

Grabbing a tissue, I clean myself up then hit print on the close-up image.

The printer whirs to life, sucking in a piece of top-grade photographic paper. Slowly, Heather's image appears on the paper, close up and glossy.

Taking it by the corners so I won't leave finger-prints on her face, I scan the wall for a place to pin it.

My computer desk and printer take up one side of the rectangular-shaped basement, where the wall is covered in photos from the first time I saw her on the hike.

Turning slowly, I search for a space on the other walls in the room. There are images of her walking in town, at work through the glass, and—my favorite—in her bedroom.

I'm good at hiding, and I'm patient. Once I found out where Heather lived, it was easy to find a place to hide in the trees around the house she shares with her parents. There's a tree with big branches and bushy leaves that has the perfect view of her bedroom.

They're my favorite pictures: Heather sitting on her bed with a magazine spread out before her, hair falling loosely over her shoulders; Heather dressing, her bare shoulders reflected in the round dressing table mirror; then a shot of her reaching up and shutting the curtains. Shutting me out.

My chest tightens. I'm tired of being on the outside looking in. I want to be with her. I want to be by her side. The two of us together, shutting the curtains on the rest of the world.

I think back to today and the man flirting with her at the cafe. After he got his coffee, I followed him and let him know with my fists that she's mine.

He won't bother her again, but others might.

My fists clench just thinking about it. It's not enough any longer to watch Heather. It's time to claim her.

There's a bare spot on the wall in between a photo of Heather in her short pajamas and one of her laughing with her friend. I pin the new picture over her friend's face. It's only Heather I'm interested in. Only Heather that's mine.

The walls are almost full, but I'm not done. I'll never be done photographing Heather.

I make a mental note to pick up some string and small pegs so I can hang photos in rows across the walls.

Switching off the light, I climb the stairs, lock the door, and slip the key in my pocket.

When I moved to Maple Falls, I bought a small property with a simple cabin and space to build a studio.

No one must ever see what's in the basement, especially not Heather.

3

HEATHER

"Hello, kitty."

The neighbor's cat is always hanging around our driveway, and I give it a scratch behind the ears like I do every morning. It meows and rubs against my leg.

When I stand up, my breath hitches in my throat. Kane is walking along the sidewalk coming toward our house. He's as hot as ever with his hair ruffled and his beard unkempt. God, how I long to run my fingers through that beard, to feel it scratch against my thighs.

"Hi," he calls out, looking surprised to see me.

He's got his camera bag slung over his shoulder. I've never seen him without it. What he finds so interesting to photograph in Maple Falls, I have no idea.

He slows down, and I join him on the sidewalk.

"I'm on my way to work."

Every time I'm near him, my knees go weak and my

heart hammers in my ears. It's so loud I'm sure he must hear it.

"I'll walk with you," he says.

We fall into step together, and he's so close I have an urge to touch him, to clasp his hand in mine.

I reach my pinkie out until it grazes his hand, and I pull away quickly, pretending it was an accident. He'd think I was weird if I tried to hold his hand. The fat, desperate cafe girl trying her luck with every new guy that comes to town.

Except it's only him. Only him who has ever had this effect on me.

"What you photographing today?"

"The sunrise," he says vaguely. "But I'm looking for something more interesting to shoot."

I have no idea what a nature photographer finds interesting.

"Like what?"

"Like you."

I give a nervous laugh. It's the same joke he tried yesterday.

"You already said that."

"How about tomorrow?"

I turn to stare at him, wondering what the hell he's talking about. He's looking at me intensely, no sign of a joke on his face.

"Tomorrow what?"

"How about you come to my studio tomorrow and let me photograph you."

My mouth drops open. He's got to be joking with me.

"Are you serious?"

"Of course." His pale eyes bore into mine so intensely that I almost believe him.

"Why do you want to photograph me?"

"Because you're beautiful, Heather."

Now I know he must be completely delusional.

I laugh. "Of all the girls in Maple Falls, you want to photograph the chubby one?"

He runs a hand through his hair and looks frustrated. "I wish you wouldn't say that about yourself. Let me photograph you, and I'll show you how beautiful you are."

His words touch a place deep inside of me, making me pause. I've never thought of myself as beautiful. I'm shaped differently than any woman I've ever seen in a magazine. But what if he's right? What if he could make me feel like one of those models? Beautiful and desired.

I have a sudden thought and my eyes narrow. Maybe he's one of "those" photographers.

"You don't mean nude, do you?"

His pupils dilate and his eyes widen. A look of pure desire crosses his face. He takes a step closer to me, his gaze dipping to my chest and back to my eyes.

"Not unless you want me to."

Holy crap. A zing of heat zaps through my body, and there's a gush of dampness between my legs.

"I'll see you at ten," he says as if it's a done deal. "Bring a few different outfits."

I swallow hard. My body's overheating just thinking about posing nude for him even though that's not what he's asking.

We reach the convenience shop on the edge of the main street, and he pauses.

"I need to grab a few groceries."

He ducks into the shop, leaving me to wonder what the hell I just agreed to and why my body's having such a delicious reaction to it.

4

KANE

My lens roves over Heather's body, taking in every inch of her. She's poised on the edge of a stool, one leg touching the floor, the other bent onto the railing. Her hands rest in her lap, playing with the tassel on her over-sized knitted sweater.

"Is it okay sitting like this, or…"

She's self-conscious and nervous in front of the camera.

"You look beautiful. Relax your hands and try a few poses."

She leans back on the stool, which pushes her breasts out. Two perfect mounds straining under her sweater.

"Like this?" She pulls a face and wraps her arms around her body self-consciously. "I've never been photographed before; I don't know what to do."

Oh, but she has been photographed before—many, many times, in many poses. Only she doesn't know it.

Setting my camera down, I walk toward her.

"Just be yourself, pretend the camera isn't here."

She pulls a face. "It's hard. I feel frumpy."

This woman is anything but frumpy, and I'm going to show her just how beautiful she is.

"What have you got on under here?" I lift the edge of her sweater, resisting the urge to yank it off.

"Just a top."

"Let's see."

She pulls the sweater over her head to reveal a tight t-shirt. It hugs her body, showing off every curve.

"It kinda shows the fat rolls through."

I fix her with a severe look. "I don't want to hear you talk like that."

It comes out harsher than I mean it to, and she looks startled.

"You have a beautiful body, Heather."

Her eyes are wide as she looks up at me, and I can't resist touching her. My hand rests on her shoulder and runs down her arm.

"Every curve is beautiful." My fingers run over her stomach. "Every dip adds to your character…" I trail them up her rib cage. "Every part of this body is a piece of art."

My fingers stop just under her breasts, twitching to go further. But she hasn't realized she's mine yet, and I don't want to scare her too soon.

Her chest is heaving up and down, and when I raise my eyes, she's staring right back at me. Her back arches, and she drops one shoulder. Her gaze makes the blood rush to my dick.

"Stay there. Right there."

Backing away, I grab the camera and start shooting.

Her penetrating gaze follows me down the lens.

"That's it, Heather. You're beautiful."

She pivots on the stool so that she's sitting sideways. Tilting her head, she drops the other shoulder and throws a bold look to the camera.

"You look gorgeous."

My finger clicks image after image. She's got the hang of it now, throwing sexy looks and tossing her hair.

"That's it, baby girl."

My words must encourage her because she swivels on the stool so she's front on. Both of her feet come up on the rail, and she slides them open as she leans forward, placing her hands between her thighs on the stool.

Holy shit. The blood pounds in my ears, and my cock pushes hard against my jeans. It's a bold pose, her legs open and her hands between them, shielding her special place, her face tilted upward defiantly.

How I long to push my way between those thighs and fuck her until she's begging for mercy.

I know I'll be wanking to these images for a long time.

"You're so sexy, Heather."

She bites her lower lip, and I almost come undone. My camera drops to my side as I feast my eyes on her.

Her expression changes, and she becomes self-conscious again.

"Was that, okay?"

My chest is heaving, and my cock aches.

"That was more than okay, honey. That was sexy as fuck. You're amazing."

She smiles shyly.

"I, um, have another outfit I thought we could try. If you have the time."

I've got all the time in the world for this woman.

"Sure."

While she gets changed, I change lenses. I'm going to want to get some close-ups. With the camera ready, I wait for her to come out from behind the changing screen. When she does, my jaw hits the floor.

She's wearing nothing but a black lacey negligee.

5

HEATHER

My arms hug my body as I step out from behind the screen. I've never done anything like this before. But Kane makes me feel safe, and he makes me feel like maybe, just maybe, I'm not as hideous as I think I am.

His mouth drops open when he sees me, and I wonder if I've gone too far, coming out in a negligee and high heels.

"Is it too much?"

He shakes his head, and when he speaks, his voice is croaky.

"Oh, baby, let me look at you."

I drop my arms, and his gaze sweeps over my body. The lace fabric grazes my skin, making me feel sexy, making me feel alive.

I stand up straighter, letting him take in my thick

thighs and heavy breasts. His gaze takes in every inch of me, making my skin burn with desire.

"Sit on the stool."

He picks up his camera, a determined look on his face.

"I want to capture you like this. You're perfect."

His words make me feel bold, confident. And for the first time, I feel like there's nothing wrong with my body. If a man like Kane can find beauty in me, then maybe I can too.

The negligee gathers under my breasts and fans out in sheer fabric, covering my stomach rolls and accentuating my wide hips. The panties underneath are matching black lace, and there's not much to them.

As I perch on the stool, I tuck one high-heeled foot onto the rail, leaving the other one on the ground. Kane licks his lips, and I wonder how much he likes what he sees.

He runs a hand through his hair, and I can tell he's flustered. The thought that I'm turning him on makes me feel powerful, confident.

As he picks up the camera, I lean forward, giving my best sexy look down the lens.

He snaps some pictures, and I turn to try a different pose. This time I lean my arms on the stool and tilt my head back so my hair falls down my back and my breasts are pushed into the air.

"Oh, Heather."

Kane groans, and the noise calls to something deep

inside off me. My core tightens, and there's a rush of heat between my legs.

The strap of my negligee slides off my shoulders, and I let it slip, throwing a confident look at the camera—at Kane.

He's breathing hard, and there's a lump in his jeans telling me just how turned on he is.

I love that I'm doing that to him.

Feeling sexy and bold, I slide the strap right off my shoulder until the soft flesh of my breast is exposed.

"God, you're sexy."

His voice is a low growl, and it makes my pussy gush. There's a pull in my core that I can't ignore.

I fix my stare down the lens as I slide my hand into my negligee.

Kane groans, a guttural voice that makes my nipples hard. "Oh, baby, you're turning me on."

My fingers run over the hard bud of my nipple, sending waves of heat through my body. My head tilts back as I fondle myself to the sound of the camera clicking. I've never felt so sexy before, never felt so bold or so turned on.

"Kane."

"Yes, baby?"

"Are these photos just for you?"

"No one else will see you." He says it with such force that I believe him. "Your body is mine, Heather. No one else will see you but me."

He growls the words, sending a shudder right

through me. He's talking possessively, like he owns me. It should scare me, but it turns me on even more.

So much so that I have to pivot on the stool to get my balance.

"You're mine, Heather. Since the moment I saw you."

The words tug at my core and fill me with need. All the while he keeps his camera raised, clicking away at my body. My sexy body.

My hand runs down my breasts and over my stomach. The negligee falls open, and I run my hand over my damp panties.

"Do you want to photograph this?" My palm cups my mound. There's no mistaking my meaning.

I don't know what's making me so bold, but it seems right in the moment. The click of the camera pauses, and he takes a sharp breath.

"Oh, baby, you don't know how much."

My hand slides into my panties, my fingers finding my soft glistening folds.

"Holy fuck," Kane growls, and he steps closer, the camera zooming in on my hand. "Take the panties off."

My thumbs hook over the fabric, and I pull them down my legs. My heart beats wildly. I don't know why I'm doing this, but I can't stop. I want him to see me. I want him to watch me down his lens.

My hands slide up my thighs to my wet pussy folds. My palm circles my hard nub, applying just the right amount of pressure.

"You're so fucking sexy, Heather."

The camera clicks, and I part my thighs, letting the lens in, letting Kane in.

"I feel sexy. You make me feel sexy."

My fingers, slick with pussy juice, rub against my clit as my other hand teases my left nipple.

The camera moves to my chest. My face. He moves around me, taking pictures from every angle.

"You're so fucking gorgeous."

My palm rubs my clit, and I let my eyes roll backwards, the soft click of the camera spurring me on toward my climax.

"I'm going to fuck you after this, Heather."

The words are like a shock wave ripping through me.

"I'm going to fuck that little pussy so hard. Show you that you're mine."

The dirty words bring me close to the edge.

"Kane."

I cry out as I reach my peak, pressing my palm against myself as waves of orgasm rush over me. The clicking intensifies, and he's photographing my face, my body, my pussy. My whole body trembles under the gaze of his lens.

When I open my eyes, the camera is at his side, and he's looking at me with an intensity that almost makes me come again.

"You're fucking beautiful."

And for the first time, I believe him.

6

KANE

Her chest is heaving, and there's a line of perspiration on her breasts. The scent of her fills my nostrils as she slides her hand down her thighs.

"That was fucking amazing."

It's a wonder I didn't come in my pants. The pictures I've taken will keep me wanking for the rest of my days.

She's breathing heavily, and her pussy is glistening and swollen, calling to my cock. Setting the camera down, I take her by the hands and pull her off the stool.

"Heather, I've wanted you since the first day I saw you."

She smiles shyly, which touches my heart. After what she just did, she can still feel shy around me. "So have I. That first day you came into the coffee shop."

I don't tell her that wasn't the first day I saw her. I'd

27

already been following her for a week. There was already a wall of pictures of her in my basement.

Leading her over to the sofa, I pull her down onto the soft rug. She lies beneath me as beautiful in the flesh as she is through the lens.

"It's time you were mine."

My cock's aching in my pants, and I shrug them off. Her eyes widen at the sight of my cock, already hard and dripping.

I run my hand over her thighs, slick with her juice.

"Get on your knees."

She does as she's told, and I lean her over the coffee table. There's a full-length mirror on the wall in front of us so I can still see her face.

It's her face that I watch as I flick the sheer fabric of her negligee up and spilt her ass cheeks apart.

She lifts her hips, and my cock runs over her entrance, wet and ready for me. My hand reaches around the front to cup her breast, my thumb grazing her nipple.

With one hand on her tit and the other on her ass, I can control her; and that's what I do now, sliding her down my shaft one inch at a time, watching her eyes widen in the mirror.

"Kane," she says breathlessly, "it's too much."

Her pussy is squeezing me tight, and I stop, letting her adjust. "You want me to stop?"

I slide out, and she whimpers. "No, don't stop."

It's the sweetest sound—a sound I've imagined too

many times. I must hear it again. My dick slides right out of her, resting the tip in her entrance.

"No, please, don't stop. I can take it."

Holy fuck, that begging is going to be my undoing. "You think you can take it, little girl?"

"I can take it. Give it to me, please."

She has no idea what she's doing to me. Her dirty words make my whole body howl.

Pulling her toward me, my dick sinks into her, just an inch, and then slides out.

"Please, Kane. Please fuck me."

Her eyes meet mine as she says it. Pleading eyes. "Please, I can take it."

Her pouting mouth saying such dirty things unleashes something animalistic inside of me.

I grab her ass and slam myself inside of her. "Take it, little girl. Take all of it."

My balls slap against her, and she cries out, her face contorting in pain that turns instantly to pleasure.

"You want it all, you take it all. Take it like a good little girl." I thrust into her, clawing at her breasts as I sink myself into her pussy.

I've waited weeks for this moment, and it's as sweet as I imagined, sweeter because now she's moaning in a high-pitched way as I slam my cock into her.

I straighten up and tilt her hips upward, allowing my cock to go deeper. She makes a guttural sound as my balls slap against her.

"Please," she pants. "Fuck me hard."

"This not hard enough for you?"

My cock pumps in and out of her, each time pulling me toward my climax. She's fondling herself between her legs as I slam into her.

The pressure builds in my balls, and I'm not going to last much longer. She meets my eyes in the mirror, and her mouth pops open as pleasure overtakes her.

She screams my name. Her pussy contracts around me, sucking me in and tipping me over the edge.

My cum shoots out, exploding into her and shattering me into a million pieces. My seed coats her walls, claiming her as mine. All mine.

Afterwards, I pull her onto my lap, my arms wrapping around her.

I kiss her shoulders, her hair, her arms. A few hours ago, I could only look at this body through a lens. Now she's mine, and I'm never letting her go.

7

HEATHER

Three weeks later…

My fingers run over the glossy surface of the magazine, and I flip to page seventeen. I'll never get used to seeing myself in print. Yet, here I am. My first modeling job.

Kane sent some of the pictures of me—not the intimate ones—to a plus size agency, and they found me work right away.

Who knew being too tall and chunky would make me a good candidate for modeling? Plus size seems to be on trend, and I've got another job booked next week in Portland.

Kane came with me to my first job, watching protectively from the sidelines.

He made it clear to the agency that it's fashion clothing only, no underwear and no swimsuits, which is fine by me. I'm happy to keep those shoots for Kane's eyes only.

In the three weeks since I've moved in with him, we've done several private shoots. I love Kane watching me through the lens. I feel so safe with him, and I feel so safe here.

My eyes stray to the basement door that he keeps locked. Kane told me he keeps his old photography kit with expensive vintage cameras down there, which is why he keeps it locked. But he looked away when he said it, and it makes me wonder if he's hiding something.

Laying the magazine on the couch, I pad over to the basement door. The handle is cool to the touch as I fold my hand around it and gently turn.

The door doesn't budge. As always, it's locked.

It could be true that he keeps his expensive camera kit down there, but this is Maple Falls; the last burglary we had was probably in the 90s. It's weird that he's so protective of it. And he's never offered to show me. I've been living here for three weeks and not once have I been in the basement.

I run my hand through my hair, and my finger catches on a hair pin. I pause, remembering the Nancy Drew books I used to love.

Pulling the hair pin out, I straighten it and slide it into the lock. My heart thumps against my ribs as I rattle it in the lock. I'm not quite sure what I'm supposed to do, but I feel the pin catch on something.

Carefully, I turn it until I hear the lock click. I pull the pin out, and when I try the door, it swings open.

There's a staircase leading down to a dark basement. My heart's thumping in my chest, and I put my foot on the first step.

I pause. Kane kept this door locked for a reason. He doesn't want anyone in here. But if I'm going to live with this man, there can't be any secrets.

I'm sure whatever it is he's hiding is harmless, but I must know.

The stairs creak as I descend into the darkness.

There's the outline of a desk with a computer and office equipment on it. So far, so harmless.

Fumbling for the switch, I turn on the light. It takes a moment for me to realize what I'm seeing. And when I do, my heart goes still.

Plastered across the walls are pictures, photos blown up large and printed, and they're all of me. All of them.

My hands go to my mouth. There are pictures of me through the cafe window, pictures of me out hiking, pictures of me in the bar with Ursula—but she's been cut out of the photos.

Slowly, I turn around. Every wall in the room is covered in my picture. They're hanging from pegs on strings across the walls. Everywhere I turn is my face staring back at me.

Then I see something that makes me gasp.

Pictures of me at home, in my bedroom, taken

through the window. I'm on my bed flicking through a magazine. I'm getting dressed. There's one where I'm sleeping. It must have been the night when it was too hot to shut the window.

My heart's racing, and my mind's in a whirl. Kane was stalking me before we hooked up. He was taking pictures of me without me knowing.

My knees give out, and I sink to the floor. Everything I thought we had, everything I thought he was, is a lie.

There's a creaking noise and footsteps on the stairs. I turn around as Kane comes down the stairs. His face is pale, his expression a picture of devastation.

"Kane," I whisper. "What…?" But I can't get the words out. I don't know what to say.

"I can explain." He crouches next to me, reaches out a hand for me. But I pull away, barely registering the hurt in his face.

"From the moment I saw you, Heather, it was like time stood still."

His pale eyes stare at me, imploring me to understand.

"You're beautiful. You're the most beautiful thing I've ever seen. And I wanted to capture that beauty."

His eyes are pleading with me, but I can't comfort him right now. I'm in shock.

I scan the room, and that's when I see them. Hanging in rows hung up by pegs. The shots from our first photo shoot.

Me pulling on my nipple. My hand rubbing myself. My neck stretched out and my face contorted in ecstasy.

I rise onto my knees and stare at the images. They're so raw, so powerful. Is that beautiful, confident woman really me?

"You're so fucking perfect, Heather."

He's so earnest, and this time when he reaches for me, I let him.

"I love you so much. I know this is weird, and I can't explain it. But when I first saw you, I had to photograph you, to find out all about you."

I should be running a mile; I should pack my bags and leave. But I don't. Because what he's saying makes some kind of stupid sense.

As I scan the photos from that first shoot, photos of me looking so confident and sexy, I remember that feeling. Kane made me feel that. He made me believe I'm beautiful.

As I look at those pictures—my chest pressed forward, my lips parted, my thighs opened—I feel a pull in my core, a flame igniting between my legs.

I have power over this man. I can bring him to his knees, and that's powerful.

8

KANE

The hurt and confusion on her face pull at my heart and make me hate myself for making her feel this way.

"Heather..." I want to hold her, to comfort her, but she pulls away. "Baby girl. You've got this hold over me."

She's staring straight ahead, and I follow her gaze. It's the images of her on that first photo shoot when she touched herself.

The photos show her in different poses, giving herself pleasure. My dick stirs to life as it always does when I look at those images. They're forever burned into my retinas.

My hand rests on her shoulder, and this time she doesn't pull away.

"You're so fucking beautiful. I wanted you to see it too."

My hand travels down her shoulder to her waist.

"You're perfect baby, just perfect."

She spins around, and her sadness has been replaced by something else, something raw and wild.

"You made me see that about myself."

Her eyes scan mine, searching for something, and I hope she can see I'm baring my soul, offering it all up to her.

"I love you, baby."

Her gaze darts back to the photos. "They're sexy, aren't they?" Her voice is barely a whisper. She's breathing deeply, almost panting.

"That's because you're sexy."

We're both kneeling on the floor, and I run my hand down her body, sliding it between her legs. She moans, never taking her eyes off the photos.

"Kane…"

I let out a breath I didn't know I was holding. Does this mean I'm forgiven?

When she turns to me, her eyes are dark with desire.

"You saw something in me that I didn't see myself."

Her hands run up my chest, causing heat to rip through my body. "You made me feel beautiful, sexy."

She whispers the words into my ear as her fingers undo my buttons.

"Because you are beautiful."

Her hands peel my shirt off, and she reaches for my jeans.

"With you I'm sexy. Only you make me feel this way."

She's pulling frantically at my jeans, and I help her pull them off along with my underpants. Flipping her skirt up, I pull at her panties, tearing them off. My hand runs over her pussy, and she's dripping wet.

She pushes my chest, pushing me backwards and onto the floor.

"I want to ride you."

The concrete's hard on my back, but I don't care. My cock's stiff and dripping as she straddles me and hoists her skirt up.

Taking my cock in her hand, she guides me into her pussy, and I slide into paradise.

Her eyes stay on the photos, and I love the fact she's getting off on herself. I stare at her images surrounding me, but nothing beats the sight in front of my eyes: Heather riding me, her lips parted as she grinds into my hips.

"Heather," I gasp, "I love you."

She pushes herself against me, riding me hard until her orgasm overtakes her. I explode at the same time, coating her insides with my juice.

She collapses on top of me, and I hold her panting body in my arms.

"I'll take them down if you want. But I can't stop watching you."

She sits up so I can see her face.

"No. I don't want you to stop. You make me feel sexy and confident. I love you."

We cling together. It's a strange love. Others might not understand it, but it's ours.

Six years later…

The sheer fabric falls away as I turn, revealing the round bump of my belly.

Click

My hands run over the taut skin where the baby inside me is growing, and I look down at it, a smile playing on my lips.

Click

"That's the shot."

My gaze finds the lens as Kane keeps shooting.

We're in the studio attached to the house where Kane does most of his work. He's made a name for himself as a portrait photographer. Customers come up from nearby towns for baby photos, family photos, and maternity shoots.

Kane doesn't just work in the studio; he also takes

his clients outside, into nature. He gets some stunning shots with the mountain landscape.

Occasionally, he disappears into the mountain for a day or two on assignment to photograph the wildlife. But he doesn't like to be away from his family for long.

My modelling career took off, and for a few years, we traveled together doing photo shoots all over the country. It didn't stop once I had kids either. That's the beauty of being a plus size model—it's less restrictive on your body.

"Lean back on the chair," Kane instructs.

I've had maternity photos done for all my babies, and they hang proudly on the wall of the studio.

Kane still loves photographing me, and framed photos of me cover the walls of our house. There's some of the kids too, and I insisted on putting him up on the wall as well.

The X-rated photos we keep for our own private collection. Once the kids are in bed, we unlock the cabinet and pull out the stash of secret dirty photos. Looking through them always leads to quick, urgent sex, the kind where we can't get enough of each other.

Just thinking about those photos makes my core ache. I'm always horny at this stage of pregnancy. As Kane clicks the camera, I slide my hand over my swollen breasts.

They're engorged and aching, the nipples so sensitive. I only have to brush them lightly and they're standing on end.

"Oh, baby girl," Kane groans.

"You got enough nice pictures," I say, my hand sliding down my body. "Now it's time for the dirty ones."

My hand runs over my tummy and down to my panties. They're already dripping wet, and I open my thighs. As my fingers run over my damp panties, the camera clicks.

———

MEN OF MAPLE MOUNTAIN

Complete the Men of Maple Mountain series for your swoon worthy OTT alphas.

Each book is a standalone but best enjoyed in together.

Men of Maple Mountain

Mountain Man's Obsession – Colette & Bear

Mountain Man's Captive – Annie & Colton

Mountain Man's Virgin – Brooklyn & Chase

Mountain Man's Muse – Heather & Kane

Mountain Man's Redemption – Bethany & Ewan

Mountain Man's First Time – Ursula & Kit

Companion titles

Mountain Man's Healer - Jenny & Rowan

All the Scars we Cannot See - Emily & Sam

Boxset Collection

Men of Maple Mountain Books 1-7

Includes a bonus short story:

Mountain Man's Steamy Anniversary - (Bear & Colette)

WHAT TO READ NEXT

THE SEAL'S OBSESSION

My skin prickles. My hair stands on end. I'm being watched. Again...

I'm married to my country; the life of a Navy SEAL is a single man's life. Then I meet Lina...

I can't give her a normal relationship like she deserves, so it's better to watch her from afar.

I follow her, collecting intel and building my dossier.

Until she catches me.

We share one passionate weekend together before I'm deployed.

When I return, she's carrying a surprise that threatens to spin my whole world around...

The SEAL's Obsession is a soft stalker, secret baby, military romance. Featuring an OTT obsessed alpha male and a sassy curvy girl.

Keep reading for an exclusive excerpt or visit:
mybook.to/TheSealsObsession

THE SEAL'S OBSESSION

CHAPTER ONE

Trent

The sound of squealing children hits my ears as soon as I get out of the pickup. I grab the box of beers and the birthday present out of the back and brace myself for the onslaught.

With trepidation, I pull open the wooden gate that leads to my brother Jake and his wife Fiona's backyard.

The scene that greets me is almost as chaotic as my last tour in Afghanistan.

Children race across the garden chasing iridescent bubbles from a machine whirring in the corner. In the middle of the yard is a tapestry of picnic blankets where women sit as babies crawl over them, pulling at hair and chewing on whatever they can find. At least two of them are crying, and one kid is sitting on the edge of the blanket, happily shoveling dirt into its mouth.

My throat turns dry. A dull ache starts in my head. Nah, Afghanistan was never this bad. I take a step backward and am about to quietly close the gate when Jake sees me.

"Trent!" He strides across the yard, wielding BBQ tongs and wearing an apron that says, "Stand back, Dad's grilling."

At the mention of my name, our other brother Nick looks up from where he's helping his eighteen-month-old son walk across the paving stones.

"I didn't know you were back."

He scoops my nephew up in his arms and makes his way over to me, his son bouncing happily on his hip.

I swallow hard. They're closing in, and escape is looking less likely but still possible.

"Just stopping by to drop the present off."

I hold up the stuffed toy wrapped in gold Christmas paper, which was all I had in the house.

"You gotta come in and see the birthday girl."

Jake's grin gives away how proud he is of his one-year-old daughter.

I give a wild look around the yard, trying to think of an excuse not to come in. My glance comes to rest on my youngest brother, Davis, who's sitting on the edge of the deck, his arm firmly wrapped around his wife, whose belly is protruding way more than it should.

Damn. My brothers have turned into breeding machines all of a sudden, and they all look happy. Poor bastards.

"Trent!"

My mother appears from inside the house and makes a beeline to where I'm still lurking half in and half out of the gate. "I'm so glad you could make it."

And there goes my last hope of escape. There's no way I can let my mother down, not when I haven't seen her in three months.

Stepping across the threshold and into the garden, I let my mom hug me and my brothers slap me on the back. I dutifully pat my nephews and nieces on their heads and let the party pull me in.

Colorful balloons decorate the garden, and a bright red balloon in the shape of a "1" is tied to the BBQ.

"Where did all the kids come from?" I ask Jake, wincing as a baby gives a particularly loud wail.

"Half of them are your family, man."

I recognize Riley, Jake's oldest, running past with a cupcake in her hands, chased by an older boy I don't recognize. But that still doesn't account for the rest of them.

"Fiona's baby group," Jake explains, "and some of my buddies that have kids."

I grab the cold beer Jake offers me and take a huge gulp, calculating how long I need to stay to be polite and not let my family down.

I reckon if I can have a good catch up with Mom,

then I should be able to retreat in about twenty minutes.

"I can't stay too long," I tell Jake. "Just got back yesterday, and I need to get supplies."

Jake looks disappointed, and I feel bad. I haven't seen my family in months.

"You gotta stay for the cake. Fiona's made a cake in the shape of a fish. You've got to see it."

I frown at my brother. Since when did he get so excited about a fucking fish cake?

"Fatherhood's really done a number on you, hasn't it?"

He shakes his head slowly. "You've got no idea, man."

But he's happy, the happiest I've seen him in a long time, so I guess that means something.

Mom perches next to me on the low wall that encloses the BBQ area. She's sipping a small glass of something red and sweet smelling. Her eyes scan the garden proudly, the family matriarch always with an eye on her children and grandchildren.

"When did you get back?" Mom asks.

"Late last night."

My family is used to my erratic schedule. As a Navy SEAL, I can be called away on short notice and be gone for weeks or even months.

It drove Mom crazy with worry at first, but she's gotten used to it over the years. She's learned not to ask too many questions about my deployments.

I tell her the few details that I can, then turn the conversation to her, asking what she's been up to, how her garden's going, what's the latest gossip from the neighborhood.

Dad comes out to the garden carrying a tumbler of bourbon.

"So many kids," he mumbles, taking a large gulp. "And now Davis has one on the way."

Dad shakes his head and makes a tsking sound. "Didn't we teach you boys anything about birth control?"

Mom hits him playfully on the shoulder. "We were the same at their age, dear."

Dad gives her a sly wink. "Oh, we were worse, sweetheart."

His hand snakes out to grab her bottom. She gives a surprised shriek and giggles like a girl. Their heads butt together as they laugh at some shared memory from almost forty years of a happy marriage.

I gulp my beer down and head inside. The last thing I want to see is my parents flirting with each other. Christ, it's bad enough all my brothers are at it.

I head to the kitchen, hoping to find the bourbon that Dad's knocking back. I don't usually drink a lot, but if I've promised to stay 'til the cake comes out, I'm going to need something stronger than a couple of beers.

It's quieter inside, without the babies and children.

I make my way to the kitchen and find the bourbon

bottle on the counter. Dad won't mind if I have a bit, so I grab a glass and pour myself a generous glass.

I'm leaning against the kitchen counter, watching the party through the window, when the kitchen door opens and a woman steps in.

My heartbeat comes to a stop. She's beautiful, like movie-star beautiful. Her chestnut hair hangs in soft waves over her shoulders, framing a round face with soft brown eyes.

As she steps into the kitchen, I take in her soft curves accentuated by the tight leggings she's wearing with a casual checkered shirt left half open to reveal a pair of large soft breasts pushing against her t-shirt.

My mouth goes dry, my dick stirs, and the blood pumps hot through my body.

She looks startled to see me, her eyes widening.

"I'm looking for a wine glass."

She holds up an unopened bottle and gives me a hopeful grin.

It takes a moment to get my thoughts together, and I must be looking at her like an idiot because her grin falters. She turns to the cupboards and bends down, opening one of them.

I tear my eyes away from her ass and step forward.

"They're up here." I reach for the top cupboard. My body is so close to hers I can feel the heat coming off her.

I'm a big guy—six foot three and broad. I keep my body in shape by training at the gym most days. In my line of work, I need to be physically prepared for anything.

But I'm not prepared for the feeling that overcomes me as this woman runs her eyes over me. With my arms reaching up to get her a glass, my muscles are on display, and she drinks them in.

Her tongue shoots out to lick her lips, and her pupils dilate.

Damn. She likes what she sees, I can tell. My dick goes hard as the heat of her gaze sweeps over me.

It's been a long time since I was with a woman, but suddenly I'm having thoughts of taking this one into my brother's bathroom and doing bad things to her.

There's a scream from outside, and we both look over to the window. One of the babies has fallen over, its face red and puckered as it wails. The mother rushes over and scoops the crying infant into her arms.

I look back to the woman in the kitchen, but the moment's gone. Besides, I'm reminded that if she's here, it must mean that one of those pug-faced babies outside is hers.

When I look back, she's pouring wine into her glass, filling it to the brim. She lifts the glass to her soft lips and takes a generous gulp, then another, before setting it on the counter with a contented sigh.

"I really needed that."

To keep reading visit:
mybook.to/TheSealsObsession

GET YOUR FREE BOOK

Sign up to the Sadie King mailing list for a FREE book!

You'll be the first to hear about exclusive offers, bonus content and all the news from Sadie King.

To claim your free book visit:
www.authorsadieking.com/free

ABOUT THE AUTHOR

Sadie King is a USA Today Best Selling Author of short instalove romance.

She lives in New Zealand with her ex-military husband and raucous young son.

When she's not writing she loves catching waves with her son, running along the beach, and good wine, preferably drunk with a book in hand.

Keep in touch when you sign up for her newsletter. You'll even snag yourself a free short romance!
www.authorsadieking.com/free